THE CAKE MAKER'S DOG

BOOK 2 BRYANT BROTHERS NOVELLA SERIES

KATHLEEN PENDOLEY

For WAnita,

RIVERHAVEN BOOKS

E-book design by Fat Cat Design

E-book ISBN: 978-1-7371403-3-7

Paperback ISBN: 978-1-7371403-6-8

www.kathleenpendoley.com

❀ Created with Vellum

IF YOU OR ANYONE YOU CARE ABOUT IS A VICTIM OF DOMESTIC VIOLENCE, HELP IS AVAILABLE. CONTACT THE NATIONAL DOMESTIC VIOLENCE HOTLINE.

WWW.THEHOTLINE.ORG

(800)799-SAFE (7233)

TTY

1.800.787.3224

For underdogs and unsung heroes everywhere

1

DAN

*S*tress defines the day. The flight into Boston was as turbulent as a tsunami wave, and my greasy-haired, surly Uber driver seemed drowsy, maybe even full-blown drunk. And, now that I've snuck out of my brother's wedding to snag a calming cigarette, I discover a full-sized German Shepherd locked inside one of the wedding guests' cars. What the hell is wrong with people?

Pocketing the butt after putting it out, I check each door handle twice, finding them all locked. Without a choice on this boiling hot day, I try forcing my arm in the passenger window, rolled down a tad lower than the rest, and almost lose my fingers in the process. I can't blame the dog for defending his territory, even if I'm only trying to save him from heatstroke.

"It's okay, buddy," I tell the snarling, frothing menace. "I'll go and find your owner."

My new sister-in-law stands by the backyard gate talking to a small group of much older females in soft pastels and English-style hats, all gushing over her pretty dress and gorgeous ring.

Colleen smiles brilliantly at me as I sidle up to her side. "Hi, Dan." She sounds chipper. "Need anything?"

I nod.

She grasps my arm, waves goodbye to the ladies, and walks me rapidly towards the bar, where she grabs each of us a glass of champagne. "Thank God you came over when you did. This smile is beginning to ache. Is it still plastered on my face?" Her grin turns clownish before it finally releases its hold. Colleen swallows the alcohol like a shot.

"It's gone now. Who were those ladies?" I trade her my flute for a beer, and we clink a toast.

"From what I can gather, they're wannabe members of Jack's fan club, though nothing of the kind exists. I've married a humble man, but don't tell them. He's found lost relatives of theirs, dead and alive, through the years, and they can't sing his praises enough." She finishes the second drink, grabs a bottle of water, and we head over to the chairs beneath the canopy where guests have started dancing. "Anyway, Dan, you look angry. Can I help?"

"It's nothing I can't handle. The bride isn't responsible for anything beyond smiling pretty."

She grimaces, not quite ready to use the happy expression.

"Tell me, do you know who owns the four-door, beige sedan with rust spots on the fender?"

After a brief pause, she remembers. "Yes! That would be Clara Bishop, the cake maker's car."

"Then the furry pile of fury would be the cake maker's dog?"

"Did she bring Kristof? It's hot out."

"My thoughts exactly. You think Clara's in the kitchen?"

"Most definitely. She's planning the big reveal after putting the final touches on the frosting."

Squeezing her elbow, I assure Colleen I have it all under control. After decades of not seeing my brother Jack, it's strange to be with him and his bride on their most special day.

Colleen has such an inviting air and carries no grudge from the past, and I feel a kinship with the woman. But she's not wrong about Jack being the man of the hour. I haven't had a chance yet to gauge his true feelings about my being here— guests have surrounded him since the ceremony ended. I should probably take his open arms' greeting for the truth and get on with my mission.

As I enter the house, the cool air of the living room stops my mental wanderings and reminds me why I'm here, the hot dog baking under a birch tree.

The kitchen is pandemonium, with dinner dishes being collected, cleaned, dried, and put into plastic crates. It's easy to recognize the demarcation line between the clean and dirty areas, and I head to the side with the towering three-tiered white cake. It's beautiful and covered in a graceful sweep of sugary handmade seashells. The blush pink shade inside a conch shell is so realistic that I want to pull it off and hold it to my ear to hear the ocean tide.

"Can I help you?" A petite and curvy redheaded female pops her head out from behind the cake, frosting smeared across her pale, freckle-laden cheeks. The look in her light brown eyes is wary and worried.

I want her to look like a person who would lock a dog inside a hot car, but she seems like the girl next door, as sweet as the frosting on her pretty face. My attempt to change my expression from a frown to neutral is no use, undoubtedly why she's nervous. "I think so. Are you Clara?"

She hesitates before admitting it. "Yes. What's this about? Does Colleen need something?"

"It's about your dog, ma'am."

She looks relieved, and she shouldn't. "Oh, Kristof. He's fine. He has plenty of water, and the car windows are open for a cross breeze."

I continue to glare, not liking her casual response.

She swallows hard. "I parked in the shade."

"It's not good enough. You need to bring Kristof home or let him out somewhere safe."

She lifts both hands, one holding a spatula, the other what appears to be pearls. "I can't. I have to finish this, and then I'll get him out for a short walk." She returns to the cake, ending the discussion. Her hands work deftly, applying the gems to make it appear as though a necklace was draped over the top. If the cake tastes the way it looks, it will be incredibly decadent.

"Then I'll call the police."

"What? You can't be serious."

"Dead serious. Cars can get well over one hundred and thirty degrees on a hot day like today. I'm a veterinarian, and that dog needs to come out of the car right now!"

My yelling didn't help. Clara looks petrified, and tears well up in her eyes. "Okay. You don't have to call anybody."

I feel like a grade-A jerk, even though she's the one who put the dog in danger.

"Brandon, can you come here, please?" Clara calls to the young guy who's been watching our discussion warily.

"Can you put the rest of these down the back?" She pours the remaining white beads into his open hand and wipes gently at the outer corner of her eyes. "Right next to this starfish. In a curve, not straight." She takes off her apron before admonishing. "Don't mess it up. Not like last time." Her words are harsh, but her smile is lovely. Until she spies me watching, and the fearful look returns.

"You got it, boss. Note to self: If I push hard enough, the cake tips over."

We both watch her flee.

In a low voice, Brandon tells me in no uncertain terms, "If you ever speak to her like that again, I'll kick your ass back to wherever the hell you came from, mister. Got it?" His dark eyes are hard granite. I have no doubt he means what he says. But, even though he's half my age, I don't believe he could do it. Thin as a rail post, Brandon seems to struggle with the simple act of applying the pearls into the thick frosting.

"Yeah, I've got it, kid." As I turn to leave, he grabs me by the wrist. I have to hand it to the boy, his grip is more crushing than expected.

"I mean it. Clara is the nicest person on the planet. She's taken enough shit from hard-ass tough guys like you to last a lifetime. Back off!"

"Clara needs to take better care of her dog." I pull my arm away from his grip, and the bastard shoves me. Instead of me losing balance, his arm rakes across the front of the cake. The gems scatter across the floor while a swath of seashells falls into an indiscernible clump, barely missing the kid's sneakers.

"Oh, shit!" he exclaims. "Clara is going to have a nervous breakdown once she sees this."

I feel responsible after talking so harshly to the lady. Now I've effectively ruined the wedding cake and, thus, the day. "Come on. Let's see if we can fix any of this. Got any more pearls or shells tucked away?"

Brandon grabs a wide canvas tote bag and begins rifling through it. He pulls out one Ziplock bag after another, and it's plain to see none of the remaining objects left in the sack are white, nor is anything from the sea.

"I guess we'll have to improvise."

Brandon's expression reflects the sick feeling in the pit of my gut as we begin to cover up the mess. I smooth down the frosting that remains with a butter knife while he opens up bags. He hands me baubles of all sizes and colors, and I pile them here and there, cascade-fashion, to match the design if not the elements. The dark red candy blends into pink, which stands in stark contrast to the blue.

"Give me some purple." Brandon tosses me the bag and walks over to look out the window.

"Well, you got your way. Clara tied Kristof to the tree and gave him a swimming-pool-sized bowl of water. He's playing with Ryder, Jack's dog." Brandon shakes his head, mumbling as he returns.

"What did you say?" I'm distracted, wondering where Clara is now and if I can finish with this emergency project before she returns.

"I said Kristof is always safe with Clara. She loves her dog and has gone out of her way to protect him."

"We don't have time to argue. Just get me the yellow things, and we can wrap this up."

He eyes my work critically. "Clara is still going to freak out. I mean, this is nothing like what she made. Hers was a masterpiece. This—" he sputters, "this is a master failure."

Clara's back.

Brandon and I close ranks and stand shoulder to shoulder in front of the mockery. "How's Kristof?" We ask together as though rehearsed.

"He might have been a little hot, but he doesn't seem any worse for the experience. He would've been fine." She sees right through us. "Show me what you're hiding."

Reluctantly, Brandon and I separate, exposing our shame.

Her eyes grow large, and her skin grows paler. "What happened?" Tears are falling down her face. Without thinking, I pull her close and try to shush away her pain. Except she's not hurt, just laughing hysterically. "Is that supposed to be a fish?" Clara points to the top decoration made with a pink, glittery sort of ingredient.

"A mermaid." I look closer and show where the flippers are. "I used these two lemon wedges for her bikini top."

She's laughing harder. Still tucked under my arm, her skin is warm and smells like caramel sugar. I try to explain the rest of my montage—a wave, a penguin, and a castle turret. Neither she nor Brandon can recognize my kind of talent.

"P-p-penguins aren't p-p-purple," she manages to get out, clutching my shirt between her fists, pressing her face deep into the material. I let them have fun before handing Clara a napkin to clean her tears after she's calm enough to step out of my embrace. It felt good having her snuggled close to me, all soft curves and feminine scents.

"What are we going to do?" She looks to me for the answer.

"I don't know. Turn it around, I guess?" I'm assuming the back of the cake has to look better than the front.

Nodding in assent, she turns her attention to Brandon. "Let's get her into the dining room. We'll move the table, and she can sit in a corner." Clara personifies the dessert, which makes her seem remarkably caring. Maybe I misjudged her from the start?

Together, the three of us have the cake adequately displayed for Colleen and Jack, ready for pictures. With their rings adorning the holder on top and the remaining perfection from Clara's expert hand, no one is any the wiser.

After helping to slice and hand out the pieces to guests, I take Clara to the side. "Hey. I'm sorry I ruined the cake. And I may have come on a little strong about the dog." We watch Kristof outside the window, panting contentedly. Between his paws lies Jack and Colleen's pup, Ryder. They enjoyed the party more than the human guests, frolicking and tousling over tennis balls and tug toys.

"I forgive you." Clara squeezes my hands.

I'm surprised at how much her simple gesture of affection stirs me.

I barely have time to blurt out, "I owe you one," to Clara, before Brandon interrupts, letting us know her car won't start.

2

DAN

"*I*t's the alternator. You'll need to have it towed." I rub my fingers clean from dirt and debris using the same old rag I did with the oil stick.

"Are you sure it isn't the battery?" Clara rips the cloth from my hand and begins wiping at the blue-green-colored acid build-up around the rusted nuts.

"Positive. We tried jumping it three times and got nothing, not even a spark. Do you have AAA?"

Her laughter is more cynical than amused. "No. I don't have AAA, a service station, or two dimes to rub together right now. All I have is my dog and this bag of sugar." She hurls the canvas tote through the driver's side window in frustration.

Kristof, who took to me quickly after he was no longer protecting his vehicle, sits in between us, his eyes focused solely on me. He thinks I'm why his mistress is angry. Unwilling to backslide in his estimation, I offer to take care of things for Clara.

She refuses. "I can't ask you to help. I don't even know your name."

"Dan Bryant." I hold out my hand for her to shake. "Jack's my brother. You have nothing to fear."

Her wary look disagrees, but she shakes on it anyway.

"We'll use my card. I'm sure Jack has a mechanic he trusts. As far as the money, we can figure something else out later." I realize how the words sound one second too late. "I don't mean anything untoward, only that I'll take care of it. It's the least I can do after the cake incident."

"I don't think that's a fair exchange. Plus, I had a different favor in mind."

Now it's my turn to wear a surprised expression. Clara's laugh at my change of face is contagious, leaving us both wiping at the tears streaming down our cheeks.

"I'm sorry." She calms enough to speak first. "It's just that I haven't had much sleep lately, and I'm a little punch-drunk. And now this." Her shoulders slump, dejected.

"It's enough to knock anybody off-kilter." I'm about to ask what wish she would like me to fulfill, and her posture turns rigid.

"We have to go. Now!" Grabbing my arm, Clara whistles one time, and Kristof follows close to our heels as she pulls me across the lawn and back inside the cottage. We catch Colleen and Jack kissing on the living room sofa. Clara slams the door behind us, breathing heavily.

Adjusting her wedding gown, Colleen innocently asks, "What's up?"

"Yeah," says Jack, "you both look like you've seen a ghost."

I'm also clueless why we had to run, and I change the subject. "About that. We still have to discuss the lineage of your wife's son."

"And we will," my brother tells me. "First thing

tomorrow morning, we'll tell you everything you need to know about Greg and how he's related to us."

Nodding in agreement, I look down at Clara, now crouching low by the front window, peeking out of the corner of the drapes. "What are you doing, Clara?"

Colleen and Jack turn to look out the same window, and Clara hisses, "Get down! He'll see you."

Through the gauze covering the leaded glass, I watch the beat-up blue car pull up beside the curb, the same make and model as Clara's. More dented and less rusted than hers, it's a hunk-a-junk on wheels.

Colleen and Jack peer out again from a safer distance. All three of them sharply inhale after seeing the man who stops in front of the house.

"Do you know who that is?" Jack asks.

"He's my ex-boyfriend," Clara mumbles.

"That's the guy who was looking for his dog!" Colleen exclaims, smacking Jack on the side. "Remember? The day we met? Ryder and I saw him at Pam's Parlor, and he looked ready for a fight."

Jack looks nauseous with his input. "That's the car that hit me, breaking my leg."

Clara's head swings towards Jack, horrified, unconsciously rubbing her wrist.

Much of the information being shared, I'm not privy to, being from out of town. But we need a plan, and these three are in a state of shock. So I decide to play hero and say, "Clara, why don't you head down into the basement with Kristof. I'll go and talk to—

"Wait. What's his name?"

"Gary."

"Okay. Colleen and Jack, you go back out with your guests and call the police. I'll keep Gary busy."

The guy strolls around Clara's clunker, cupping his hand on the window to see inside before looking over his shoulder at the house. I'm familiar enough with shady characters to know he's rotten to the marrow. Something tells me it's a good thing Brandon already left or he'd be out there confronting Gary—the kid is *very* protective.

Jack, Colleen, and Clara follow my directives, and I head out to greet Gary. "Hi! Are you from the fix-it shop?"

"No." Gary is scruffy and surly and not interested in sticking around to talk as he heads back to his car.

"Oh." Playing mickey-the-dunce is one of my superpowers. "So you're here for the party then." That gets his attention.

"Got any beer back there?"

"Tons." I head towards the back yard and wave for him to follow. The further he is from his car, the less likely he'll flee when the cops arrive. I don't know much about this island, but I know Gary took off after the accident a year ago, leaving my brother by the side of the road like trash. It's high time Gary pays for his crime.

The first thing I noticed about Jack was his marked limp. He never had one before, and as we sat down to dinner, I blurted the question. "What the hell happened to your leg?" Who would have thought the perpetrator would be in our midst so soon after?

Gary and I round the corner to the back yard, and a police cruiser turns down the lane. "So, are you a lager man or whatever's cold?" I ask, angling myself so Gary's back faces the street.

"Doesn't even have to be cold as long as it's wet. Am I right?" He tries to give me a fist bump while I struggle against the desire to knock his block off. That he's crude isn't a surprise, but expecting me to act like his buddy is a bit much.

Colleen and Jack sneak back inside to meet with the officer at the front door. It shouldn't be long before they come take this jerk off my hands.

After I hand him the cheapest beer brand available, Gary pops the top and has it half empty in seconds. "That hits the spot. Got another?" He crushes the can in his fist and drops it on the grass. His gaze fixates on a group of young women—women too young to be ogled that way. Hell, no age is appropriate for a man to be looking at any woman the way Gary is right now, the lech.

"Watch yourself, pal. I invited you in for a drink, not to make trouble."

He scoffs at my remark and reaches into the cooler to help himself. "I'm just soaking in the sights. No need to get jealous, buddy. I see enough hotties to go around." He cracks open the top, oblivious to my fists clenched by my side or the tall police officer approaching from behind.

"Gary Tierney?"

Gary keeps chugging without bothering to turn around. Once he's had his fill, he belches and asks, "Who wants to know?" He wants another fist bump and remains hanging.

"I'm Officer Franklin. I'm going to have to take you in for questioning about an accident last April. The charge is for fleeing the scene after causing bodily injury to a pedestrian."

"Wasn't me." Gary continues to drink.

"Either come with me peacefully, or I can arrest you. I'll give you five seconds to decide."

Gary smashes and tosses his second beer and agrees to go peacefully. It's certainly a wedding to remember.

With Gary gone, I head back inside and find the lucky bride and groom sitting once again in the living room, looking concerned. Kristof leans against Clara, who cries into a linen napkin. She flinches, feeling my hand upon her shoulder.

"Hey, are you okay?" I crouch down to her level and wipe her hair out of her face. "We'll fix it. Just tell me what it is."

Clara is incapable of speech, and Colleen answers for her. "The police have to search her apartment for evidence. Gary has a few other warrants pending for things like armed robbery and DUI's. Clara doesn't have anywhere to stay until they finish. Where it's Saturday, that won't be until Tuesday at the earliest."

"Then she can stay with me." *Why the hell did that pop out of my mouth?*

When she sobs harder, it comes back to me: I hate to see a woman cry. It tears me in two, and I want to do whatever it takes to make it stop. The sad fact is, I lost my ability to fix anything after the wildfire destroyed what I built. I hardly know what I'm doing day-to-day, and now I've offered to navigate it for someone else. Here goes nothing. "We need to get her car towed, and then we can swing by her place for clothes and stuff."

Jack rejects my plan. "No, they won't let anyone inside. She can't take anything from the place, not even dog food. We can pay for her stuff if you take her shopping for the essentials."

With the three of us lost in planning what's to become of Clara, we don't notice until she's out the door that she hadn't agreed with any of it. With the keys to Colleen's SUV in my pocket, I chase Clara, stopping her on the driveway. "What is it, Clara?"

"You're all incredibly kind." She swallows hard to eliminate the tremble in her voice. "I can't ask you to do this.

Brandon's mom will probably let me sleep on their couch." Heeling up Kristof, she continues down the street.

"How far is his place? At least let me drive you over." The ride will buy me some time to convince her my offer has no strings attached.

"About six miles." The reality of the scorching heat and the long walk seem to hit her. "Okay, you can give me a ride."

I have some fast talking to do, and I get right to it once we settle into our seats and begin driving. "I'm sorry you're going through this. I just went through hell myself, and I totally relate to how upsetting it is when things unravel." I swallow hard.

No one else knows what spurred me into responding "yes" to Colleen's wedding invite. Sure, I wanted to see my brother and had hoped that time had healed past wounds, but nothing was left to keep me in California. "My veterinary practice was near Kern County. It took me years to expand it from a two-room bungalow into a massive medical center. We offered specialists, boarding, even a doggy-daycare, on top of all the regular things people expect from their veterinarian.

"Then the fires came. We believed we'd be okay, that the fire wouldn't spread that far that fast. At least, that's what the firemen told us, and the marshal never ordered an official evacuation.

"But the last few years had been much drier than usual, and the frightening thing about wildfires is the unpredictability. It isn't like lighting a match or flicking a lighter wheel."

Man, I could seriously use a smoke right now. My heart is racing, and I have to grip the wheel like a vise to keep my hands from shaking. "It's more like a tidal wave of burning hell flooding and destroying whatever finds itself unlucky enough to be in its path.

"The clouds of smoke were growing and getting closer, so I called my own evacuation. People from other counties were exiting in droves and wanted to get their pets back, no matter where they were in the recovery process."

"I would too," Clara whispers. She pulls herself close on the bench seat and rests her hand on my thigh; it's comforting.

"Agreed. The entire staff began signing off on release forms and discharging cats, dogs, ferrets, you name it. We probably had ninety percent of the pets out, safely driving away with their caretakers, and the blow-up happened. It sounded like an explosion—which is pretty much the definition of a blow-up. A massive one, at that. The screech of the fire alarms followed, and then we were doused with the soaking jets of the sprinklers."

"Pull over, Dan." Clara shoves against my shoulder with both hands to get my attention and bring me back to reality. Sweat pours down my face, and I can't catch any air.

I signal and park in a strip mall before reaching into the glove compartment for my cigarettes. "Sorry. I need a minute." I hop out and pace and smoke and try to forget. It takes a while, and after two more cigarettes, I'm calmer.

Clara joins me outside the SUV, concern drawn on her beautiful face. "Let's revisit this another day, okay?" She leans against the driver's side door beside me, close enough to feel her hip and thigh against mine. "I'll stay with you, Dan."

The line between who needs the safe space more has just blurred.

3

CLARA

*T*he clock strikes midnight before I'm finally in my comfy clothes, brand spanking new like everything else Dan and I picked up on our spending spree. He bought me ridiculous amounts of goods—complete outfits, lacy underthings, and this terrycloth pajama short set. He makes me laugh to the point of tears and sad to the same extreme. I hope his generosity is genuine, and that he won't look for payback in a form I can't offer.

I'm thirsty as all get out, and my belly requires sustenance. I head to the kitchen to snag one of the bananas Dan picked up at the grocery store. I fear becoming a bother, and I determine only to take what's necessary, even if I do want a steak and cheese sub with all the fixings in the worst way.

Dan stands inside the cozy three-season porch, busily removing goods from a brown bag when I scurry by. We bought an awful lot of stuff today. He stops me in my tracks. "Hungry, Clara?"

"Mind-reader, Dan?"

His smile pleases me. Although he must be in his forties, maybe five years older than me, the look lends him an endearing boyish charm. "No. Just famished, and I figured the same feeling brought you out of your room finally."

It's only been a couple of hours, and lord knows it took a while to wash this day away. Plus, being out of the habit of taking tags off clothing, it took me longer than expected to get them ready for cleaning before wearing.

My nose has found a new best friend; the scent of savory goodness from an actual steak and cheese sub with a side of fries and a barrel-style crunchy pickle wafts from the sack.

"Seriously, Dan? I imagined a steak and cheese would be just the thing. Any hots on it?" Sidling up to watch him unpack the rest of the fare, I begin to drool.

"A smattering." He's inhaling deeply too. "Do you always smell like dessert?"

I shrug. "Hazard of being a baker."

"Nice perk." He hands me the meal and offers me a drink.

"Just water, please."

Kristof sits before me, waiting for his share. We've split many a meal between us when I didn't have enough money for electricity, let alone food. Gary was never good with steady work, and though Clara's Cakes has been growing every year, it still doesn't bring in enough for having all the amenities.

Now back with our drinks, Dan sits down, grabs his food, and points a pinky finger at Kristof. "Don't let him fool you. He had a huge dinner, and I took him for a walk around the neighborhood."

"Don't do that!"

Food spews from my mouth in my haste to protect Kristof.

Dan doesn't know the lengths I've gone through to hide my dog from Gary. After excusing my bad manners, I clean up the remnants of the sub that Kristof doesn't scarf down and crumple up the napkin, tossing it into the paper bag from which it came.

Dan stares at me before asking, "Why don't you want me walking Kristof?"

That he contemplates before speaking and reacting is a quality I'm unfamiliar with in men. He acts so differently from Gary, and I struggle to believe they are the same species.

I shovel perfectly spiced, crunchy fries into my mouth and talk around them. Nervous jitters have me needing a distraction and, unlike Dan, I don't smoke. "When Gary gets out—and they won't hold him long—he'll be back. He isn't looking for me. He wants his dog back." The container empties faster than expected, and I make short work on the rest of Dan's. "And that will be a problem because he'll only get Kristof after he's pried from my cold, dead hands." Without any more food to fuss with, I stroke Kristof's back in earnest. He's been my ballast through more than a few storms.

It doesn't take long before Kristof gets bored with my ministrations and ambles over to his new dog bed, his first one ever, and lies down in the corner. I'm left rubbing my wrist for comfort.

Dan grasps my hand, leaving me with no further comfort measures. "I notice you do that whenever you're nervous. Does the area hurt terribly?" He takes over where I left off, gently massaging the sensitive spots, including my palm and forearm. His calloused fingers feel decadently sensuous on my skin.

"It was the last thing Gary did. The proverbial straw that broke us up. He didn't like that I had gained some weight and was always hounding me to go on a diet. It's hard, though. My cakes taste amazing!"

He surprises me by grabbing two wrapped paper towels off the end table beside him. Opening mine, I discover a thick slice of Colleen and Jack's wedding cake. "How?"

"After taking my first bite, I knew it wouldn't be enough." He flashes me that sweet grin of his. "I stole, like, five pieces, and these are the only two left."

No words currently in the dictionary can adequately describe the feeling emanating from my heart. Gary would no more have offered me food, except for maybe a carrot stick, than he would have stopped pushing me around. He hid food from me, and whenever he brought home take-out, it was only for himself. I'd be forced to sit beside him, hungry or not, while he chowed down and got drunk. That I let Gary get away with it sickens me. Still, having a man encourage me to eat is mind-blowing. "Thanks! You don't know how much this means."

We finish the dessert in silence. Dan's casual acceptance of my need to eat convinces me that I'm safe enough to tell him the events that led up to the fracture. "The night it happened, I had just finished making a five-tier wedding cake, each layer a different flavor with a corresponding frosting. It was a thing of beauty with its rainbow effect. The size called for so much cake mix that I got confused and made extra—no big deal." I shrug. "I could use it to make a miniature version for the two of us. Gary's birthday was a few days away, and it seemed like a good excuse. Maybe then he wouldn't use it to insult my expanding waistline or my thicker-than-he-liked thighs.

"It didn't work. For some reason, possibly because I exist, Gary saw red. Kristof tried to jump in, leaping and snarling, without grabbing hold of anything. Gary kept his body protected behind the kitchen table before kicking Kristof in the head. Kristof yelped in pain and tried to shake it off. Gary took his chance, twisting my hand to get the frosting spatula out of it. We heard an audible snap, and he took off."

"He broke your arm and left you alone?"

Dan all but breathes fire, nostrils flared in anger. I would soothe him if I knew how. Gary never liked being touched unless—you know.

I carry on with my story, hoping the ending will help Dan settle down. "Gary always left after he hit me. Maybe for a few hours, sometimes a few days. He'd come crawling back and convince me it was an accident. And I believed him at the beginning. I never imagined myself in an abusive relationship. My father never hit my mother, and they never hit me. The surprise of it allowed denial to take hold."

Dan looks angrier, forcing me to talk faster.

"Anyway, I called Brandon, and his mom took me to the ER. On a positive note, it was my rock bottom. I wasn't going to take it anymore. The hardest part has been keeping Kristof hidden and safe."

The intensity of Dan's gaze becomes lethal enough for me to stop speaking.

"Are you okay?" He's not angry with me, but I don't want him blowing his stack, regardless.

His tone is calmer than expected, and his message is quite clear. "It's been decades since I've had to pummel somebody. If Gary weren't at the police station, I'd track him down and make him regret ever raising a hand to you."

The heat from his emotions seeps through our light nightwear. Instead of feeling threatened, as I would with Gary, Dan's ferocity makes me feel safe.

"Thank you, Dan. I wish I had a friend like you on my side back then." Holding his handsome face in my hands, I kiss his forehead, cooling the warm area.

He places his hands over mine and insists, "You're beautiful! Don't ever let another person tell you otherwise."

Before I can respond, he's doing the kissing, and it's a far cry from my sisterly peck. Softly at first, his mouth brushes against mine, memorizing the parameters. He prods my lips open and electrifies my tongue with a slow sensual stroke of his own. Sliding it expertly down the length of mine, he reverses his approach until he's tenderly tracing the edges of my lips with his teeth.

His voice hitches as he lets go and pushes away from me. "Maybe we should put a hold on this until we know each other better." He doesn't go far and remains close enough to hold my hand and brush the unruly hair from my face, which he does with feather-light strokes.

"Agreed." I tuck myself under his muscular bicep and rest my head on his chest. "Can you just hold me for a little while? I haven't felt this safe since I was a little girl."

"You can stay here for as long as you like. Tell me, what favor were you going to ask me?"

I laugh, having forgotten my agenda for a brief period. "I can hardly ask for anything more, could I? Food, clothes, shelter, and paying for my car to be fixed. Forget about it." I snuggle in closer, enjoying the smell of laundry detergent and light cologne.

"I won't be able to sleep unless you tell me," he teases. "I'll toss and turn, and then I'll have to make something up. What if I mess it up?"

I push myself up against his solid chest and find his maple-syrup-colored eyes watching me. They're filled with compassion, and I want to dive into their waiting depths and never have cause to worry again. "You don't strike me as a person who can make a wrong decision, Dan. But if it's going to ruin a good night's sleep, I'll tell you." Resting my body down again, I almost purr from him, squeezing me closer. "I was going to ask you to take Kristof."

"For the night?"

"No. Forever. You said you were a veterinarian." Tears threaten my eyes just thinking about letting my one true love go. "I don't want to lose him, but it's terrifying to imagine Gary discovering the truth. The lie we told him was that Kristof ran off while I was at the hospital. That he jumped through the screen after I left the front door open. I prayed Gary would give up looking for him in a few weeks. Now, it's been over a year, and he still persistently haunts me. That's why Kristof comes wherever I go, or Brandon watches him. It's too dangerous otherwise."

"What a piece of work." Dan talks into my hair. "Don't worry about a thing. We'll figure out a way to keep the both of you safe, once and for all."

With the sound of Dan's low, melodious voice, the tension from the day eases from my stiff neck and tense shoulders. Kristof snores contentedly in the corner, and, for a moment, I believe Dan's declaration.

4

DAN

"Good morning, Jack."

"Thanks for coming over, Dan." We shake hands and sit at a banquet table still set up in his back yard from the wedding. The coffee he pours smells bold, and I encourage him to fill it to the top.

"Mind if I smoke?"

"Kinda." But Jack shrugs, letting me decide.

"We're outside." The argument is weak, even to my ears. It's a nasty habit, and I understand his reluctance. What Jack doesn't understand is that I quit for six years before the fire, then lit up the minute they released me from the hospital, from third-degree burns on my legs and smoke inhalation. Stupid, no doubt, but nothing else has ever calmed me quite the same way. I'll quit again after setting a new date.

"I know. I just care about you, Dan."

"Great."

"What?"

"Now I can't smoke. The guilt would eat me alive." Being the oldest of us brothers, I still blame myself for letting one of my cubs slip away. If only reliving the night we lost

Mason was an option, things would be vastly different today. Guilt and regret weigh heavy on my shoulders, and I change the subject to avoid his pity-filled expression. "Colleen sleeping in?"

"Yeah." His expression is all dreamy-eyed and smitten. Jack always did fall harder than the rest of us. "I'll wake her in time to get ready to leave for the airport. Before we do, you and I have some things to discuss. We'll start with Greg." He holds up a finger. "Just give me a minute. First, how is Clara holding up after yesterday?"

"She's okay. Nervous and wary, but I think she's settling into the cottage nicely. When I left, she was elbow deep in making another dessert."

"Colleen has a sixth sense about who is the best match for which cottage. It's kind of strange. I'd have put you in the one-bedroom near the main drag. You're lucky she saved a two-bedroom."

I see-saw my hands. Most things can be looked at in multiple ways.

"Clara's a nice lady. You could do worse, big bro."

"Yeah. Don't go mailing the wedding invitations just yet."

Ryder bounds over and places his front paws on my knees, angling for a chin scratch. I whisper a "thank you" for the distraction, allowing me to veer the conversation in another direction. He goes back to sniffing the area for any missed food bits from last night's reception. "Is there any more news about Gary?" I can't help adding a slur to his name.

"That was the other thing. Gary is a grouch, and not in a sweet Muppet way. He pummeled his cellmate and then turned on the cops, who tried to break it up. With his other outstanding warrants, Gary shouldn't be a problem for a long time. Two of his crimes were committed in Colorado. Before long, he'll be going back to Boulder for trial. Let Clara know she can breathe a bit easier."

"What a relief! She'll be thrilled to hear." Then my mind begins to wander…Will she be able to move straight home? The police said Tuesday at the earliest, and I'm hoping that's still true. Her sweet personality has me wanting to get to know her better. And for that, we need time. "Now, before I have to slug it out of you, who the hell is Greg?" The old tagline always worked growing up whenever Gabe, Jack, or Mason stepped out of line. Translation: often for my little brothers.

"Don't even, Dan. Colleen has me running and lifting weights. She likes me fit." Smiling over the rim of his cup, Jack looks pleased with his courage in the face of my threat.

"Whatever. Fess up."

"Okay. Greg is Mason's son." He waits for me to absorb that tidbit, then continues. "Colleen was troubled in her youth, and Mason was a one-night stand she doesn't quite remember. Greg's an amazing kid. He may be Mason's, but he acts more like me."

"Well, you were pretty much the same person."

"Genetically, sure. Otherwise, complete opposites, wouldn't you say?"

"He was the fighter to your peacemaker, the wise guy to your bookworm. And, if I remember correctly, the man-whore to your virgin."

I'd said it in such a measured tone, it takes a moment for my insult to sink in. Once it does, Jack scrambles over the table and pulls me down to the ground, his arms around my neck in a sleeper hold. It feels good to tousle with one of my brothers like we did when we were young, and nothing could stop us.

Colleen comes flying out the door, calling out, "Stop! Don't hurt him!" which only adds fuel to the fire.

"You need your wife to fight your battles for you?" The smoking habit has me out of breath, and I change tactics and struggle to stand and lift him onto piggyback.

"You better watch your mouth!" Jack clutches to my back as I spin him in circles. He never had a robust constitution, and it's not long before he's begging for mercy. I'd rather not grant it, but he will puke on my head, which leaves me no choice.

Colleen rushes to his side, foolishly kissing the clear loser. "Isn't he the cutest when he gets all green around the gills like that?"

I like her even more as she razzes him for me.

"He's a button." Reaching out, I pinch his green-hued cheek.

"Does he know about Greg?"

Colleen sits while Jack fills our cups, killing the carafe of coffee. I grab a donut, the taste closer to sawdust compared to the blueberry muffins Clara whipped up before I left.

"Yes. Dan learned who Greg's dad was before he got his ass kicked."

Jack is nothing if not persistent about his narrative. He was never one to pick fights or follow through with them either, proving he was wiser than the other three of us brothers put together.

"Listen, Jack, all joking aside. I wanted to apologize for not being here sooner, for not being part of your life earlier. Gabe and I shouldn't have left, and we most certainly should never have blamed you. Mason was messed up and had a wild side that didn't care about how much he hurt people." I didn't expect to get all maudlin, but losing all you hold dear has a way of making you appreciate what's right in front of you. "I needed the space to get my head on straight. Know this: I regret how I treated you. I didn't lose one brother that day; I lost all three. I'm sorry."

Colleen wipes a tear from her eyes before passing the napkin to Jack, who hands it off to me. All that's missing is violin music.

"Thanks, Dan. I know we all react to trauma differently. It took a long time for me to make peace with all the losses in that short period. It's hardly common to lose your mother, father, and brother in less than two years."

Jack waves his hands, wiping the line of thought away. "Ever talk to Gabe?" he asks as Ryder jumps onto his lap to assist in the tear clean-up while the three cuddle close. It makes me miss Clara and our romantic moment last night on the porch.

"I haven't spoken to him since we parted ways at the airport after dad's funeral. He was getting serious about a gal down in Georgia, and I don't know what became of them. He's not listed anywhere. Maybe it's another case for Colleen." My lame joke falls flat, for we'd all like nothing more than to have us four Bryant brothers sitting around the breakfast table. A dream that can never be.

"I can keep trying," Colleen offers. "I traced Gabe to Kentucky and lost track again. Maybe he went back to Georgia. Who knows?" She clears up the few remaining mugs and plates before kissing Jack on the head. "I'm going to get ready. The car to the airport will be here at two o'clock." She blows an air kiss our way and heads back inside. "You boys enjoy catching up."

"Seriously likable lady, Jack."

"Colleen is the best thing that ever happened to me."

"Tell me more about Greg."

Jack blocks Ryder's ears and says in a low voice, "And

Greg is the second best," before holding three fingers over Ryder's furry head. It's official—I'm not the winner for the bronze place.

Jack gets lost extolling our brother's son's virtues. Greg is almost as genetically similar to Jack as he is Mason, his biological father. It blows me away how closely related they are, just like Jack and Mason were closer than Gabe and me. One egg equaling two humans. Though much of the identical twin "thing" is pure, descriptive science, there still seems a component of unquantifiable mystery.

"He just finished his freshman year on the dean's list. The kid is kind and funny and great with Ryder, and I couldn't love him more if he were my own."

"I'm happy for you, Jack." He deserves all the goodness in the world after putting up with his brothers during our formative years. He could use the exact adjectives he used to describe Greg himself. Jack has always been a cut above. "I look forward to getting to know my nephew better. Do you think he'd hang out with me now and again?"

"Are you sticking around?"

"For a short time anyway. I'm sort of in-between jobs at the moment, and I'm not sure what my next right choice is."

"Big stuff. Still helping save the lives of animals, I'm sure."

I nod though I don't share in Jack's confidence. Can I handle the responsibility after losing so much? The belief that I am no longer worthy of holding their precious lives in my destructive hands is hard to shake off.

"We'll be back from the Bahamas in ten days. Greg is on summer break, and I know he'll be thrilled to get to know you. He loves animals almost more than he loves quantum physics, and that's a lot."

"Well-rounded."

"Perfectly so."

Jack strikes me as a man who will never stop gushing about his "child," so I do it for him. "Listen, have a great time! I'll stay at least until you're back from the honeymoon. Is it okay to keep using the cottage? Bill me weekly to start, and if the vacation goes longer than a month, we'll renegotiate."

"Never! The family rate is always free. I'll sell it to you for a dollar should you ever decide to stay permanently." He pulls me into a big hug, and I know he means it. Another of his best qualities is his generous nature. Regret stings my eyes.

"I've missed you, Jack."

Hearing my voice crack, he holds on for another moment before letting me go. "Colleen and I would love to have you over for dinner. We're experts at ordering up Thai food."

"That sounds great. Enjoy the honeymoon, bro." We shake hands one final time, and I watch him walk back inside, waving as he goes.

Jonesing for a fix, my cigarette is lit before I round the corner of the house. Making amends is stressful work, and I've barely scratched the surface.

Man, the first drag feels like heaven! The love-hate cycle of this addiction keeps me in its noxious grip. The few butts that I genuinely need to appease the monkey on my back are indescribably pleasurable. They wreak havoc on my internal organs while making it feel like a surprise party in every cell of my being. Lights, glitter, and free tequila shots included.

Then there are the others. The ones I don't really crave. Those I smoke out of habit or boredom. They make me regret picking the habit back up. The dryness they create in my mouth causes my imagination to develop catastrophic scenarios of sores, tumors, and trouble. The light smokers' cough that returned shortly after lighting back up reminds me that my alveoli choke and struggle to maintain the proper oxygen saturation in my blood. Still, I keep having just one more, trying to recreate that blissful first puff, and sometimes I do. It's the hit that keeps me coming back for more.

5

DAN

"*Either* I have forgotten basic math, or there's a shit-ton more than one cake here that needs dropping off." Clara's been busy since I stepped out. One massive cake, ten dozen cupcakes, and an incredible amount of frosted and decorated brownies sit cooling on the flat surfaces in the rental. Or the freebie, as is the case with Clara and me.

"Well, I have the one wedding cake." She points to the white dessert that looks as much art as a delicacy. "That gets dropped off first. It's my simplest option, and I don't need to stick around like I did yesterday at Colleen and Jack's."

Her version of simple differs significantly from mine, with the confection's fondant frosting formed to look like two swans with necks entwined. It glistens with glittery sugar and tumbling crystals. "Then, I donate once a month to the senior center; they love my cupcakes." Her eyes dart quickly to mine before letting me know half the brownies are for me, the other half for the food pantry. "Are you sure you don't mind carting me around to all those places?"

"I don't mind at all. And thanks for the brownies." I snatch one from the tray closest to Clara, a miniature kitten face drawn on the top. "Delicious!" The proclamation hardly does the brownie justice.

"It was that or a lemon meringue pie. I had extra cocoa, so the brownies won."

"Never lemon meringue," I tell her with the seriousness of a heart attack. "That's nasty."

She pretends to write herself a reminder note of my preferences with an invisible pen and no paper.

I want to remove the frosting smeared on her cheek with my tongue and opt instead for a wet paper towel. Clara holds her breath, watching me wipe the mess away.

"I'm sorry," I warn her and close the narrow gap, separating my mouth from hers. "I have to kiss you." I wait for any sign of approval, and she doesn't hesitate before joining her lips to mine. Sweetness redefined; she tastes better than all the treats combined.

"What time should we leave?" I ask, still holding her close after kissing her thoroughly for what feels like the best five minutes of my year.

"Probably now." Disappointment replaces her look of passion, and I couldn't agree more with the sentiment. Spending a Sunday kissing this woman senseless is the only thing I feel like doing right now, but cake waits for no man.

"Just tell me how, and I'll pack it into the car."

Breaking out of our embrace, she's all business again. "Yes. No more fixing cakes for you. I'll box it all up, and you'll only need to make sure they won't topple over."

Together we make short work of packing up the backseat of the SUV and begin driving. The cake being the most crucial delivery, at least by profit standards, gets dropped off without fanfare, no decorative mermaids or creative punting necessary, and the donations are next.

The woman who lets us in at the senior center trills, "Oh,

sweetheart!" and pulls Clara into a tight embrace, rubbing her back furiously. "We weren't sure you'd make it today after hearing about Gary. Always trouble, that one. Why in grade school, he was always getting sent to the principal's office. If he wasn't talking back to the teacher, he was rolling Oreo cookies between the classrooms while they tried to teach. Once, he even stole a lunch tray and used it to sled into the teacher's parking lot. He scratched the principal's car. The sass!" The sweet lady shakes her head while Clara tries to soothe her worries.

It sounds hilarious to me, but what do I know? My three brothers and I caused a lot more trouble than cookie chaos. During recess, we got into fights, pushed each other waiting in line for lunch, and plugged up many sinks and toilets with all the bathroom paper towels available. Acting like a punk and primary education seem to go hand in hand.

Our last stop is at the food pantry behind St. Stephan's Church, the atmosphere bright and inviting, yet the shoppers don't seem thrilled to be there. Who could blame them? Food insecurity weighs on a person like no other.

It isn't until they notice the piles of boxes Clara and I are carrying in that the ladies look away from the canned goods and take an interest. Once the boxes are piled high, and the first top is cracked open, smiles spread across their faces. The attention to detail is what has them so happy.

"Look at those perfect roses!" One woman exclaims. "My dead-beat ex never brought me flowers that pretty!"

"Is that a calla lily?" a lady leaning on a cane asks. "They look delicate, like the real thing!"

"I like the puppy-dog face," exclaims a sweet little girl about seven years old.

Clara smiles graciously while the ladies sing her praises. "Thank you. I love making them especially for you. It's my pleasure." Before we go, she hands the woman operating the counter a small envelope.

I'm sick with regret. Why hadn't I pulled Clara aside on the day of the wedding and spoken diplomatically about Kristof? The opportunity to try the healthier method presents itself, and I take it by asking, "Can you afford to give stuff away for free like that?

"Not really, but it makes me happy to see other people happy. It's not much, just something I can offer."

As we drive out of the church parking lot, she jumps slightly in her seat and faces me. "I plan on paying back all the money you spent. It will take a little while, but I will. I don't want you thinking I'm giving things away and shirking my responsibility to repay my debts."

"What?" I couldn't be more surprised if she'd just told me she was a serial killer. "I didn't think anything like that. Plus, it's impressive that you share what you have."

"We should each do what we can." She's rubbing her wrist again, and I take her hand and kiss the area.

"Better?"

It feels like the sun just peeked out from a dark cloud when a beautiful smile spreads across her lovely face. "Much."

"Now, I need to try to explain why I reacted about Kristof the way I did yesterday. I had two German Shepherds, and they both died in the wildfire." I can hardly continue. Losing them that way will torture me for the rest of my time on earth, and I don't share it with most people. I can keep the emotions at bay while the experience remains hidden. For some unexplained reason, with Clara, I can't help letting it out.

"Oh, Dan. That's terrible." One of her hands gently massages my neck, and she continues to hold my available hand with her other. "Where were they?"

"I kept the bungalow that the business outgrew for my home. The medical center was a separate building. I was working, and, of course, once the smoke turned to fire, I focused on opening as many cages and doors as possible to give the animals a chance in hell at survival. Time had run out for their owners to get to them. At the same time, my house and everything outside the clinic were in flames. Without a sprinkler system in my house, it burned like a box of matchsticks. I usually brought Morgan and Manson with me, and I knew we'd be leaving the second I finished at the clinic. My car was packed with all that I cherished, including my precious pups." I see no point in hiding my tears as they're running down my cheeks, soaking the fabric of my t-shirt. "Yesterday at the wedding, I rounded the corner to sneak a smoke, and I found Kristof out in the heat—" Choking on my words, I swallow hard before continuing. "It seemed like it was all happening again. But this time—this time, I could save them. And I came off like a colossal jerk. I had no right, Clara. I'm sorry."

"Don't be, Dan." She helps to wipe my tears away while she talks. "Especially putting it that way, of course finding Kristof would be triggering. I should have found options beyond leaving him in the car, maybe asked Colleen and Jack for permission ahead of time. Anyone could see how well he got along with Ryder. In fact, Colleen mentioned setting up a playdate after they get back from the honeymoon."

"Funny that you mention it. I got a call from my nephew, Greg, on my way home. We're going to meet at the beach tomorrow for a few hours. We'd love for you and Kristof to join us."

"Are you sure? I haven't been to the beach in ages."

"Positive. We'll pack a picnic and dog treats. Ryder will be there too."

"Sounds wonderful, Dan."

"Ready for lunch?" I ask as my stomach grumbles. Reliving horror can get my appetite revved.

"A little," she answers shyly after angling her face away, covering it with the fall of her curly red tresses. The pretty spirals accentuate the profile of her sweetly turned-up little nose.

A sign on the side of the road advertising a seafood restaurant beckons, and I pull into the parking lot. "Is this place okay?"

"It's fine."

I park the car. "Have you ever eaten here?"

"Once—my first date with Gary. They serve good food at a fair price."

"Do you get paid to advertise for them?" I tease, opening her car door.

"No. It's written right on the sign."

"So it is. Are you sure you're okay with eating here? We can go someplace else if you prefer."

"No, I like the idea of creating a new memory to offset the bad."

I take her hand and we walk up to the hostess. "Two please."

Once seated on the picturesque dock, a broad blue and white striped awning overhead to protect us from the sun, I look for more information about her past.

"Where else did you and Gary go on dates?"

"Nowhere." She takes a long, nervous gulp from her water glass.

"You must have gone somewhere. A walk around the neighborhood or a movie?"

Clara shakes her head. "No. Just that one time. After that, I did all the relationship work."

"That makes no sense, Clara." She's all a man could want to hold onto and more. "He's a twit, and you're—well, you're incredible."

She blushes sweetly, smiling. It's obvious that she isn't used to compliments. "Thanks. I sold out pretty cheap, but I didn't know better."

"I hope you do now."

The waitress takes our order, and Clara tries to get away with asking for only a cup of soup.

"That isn't enough to fill anyone. Get yourself something you wouldn't typically eat. Today's a day to splurge." I look to our server and say, "We're celebrating a special occasion today."

Clara gives me a suspicious look and orders the lobster roll and fries.

I raise my glass for a toast. "Cheers." We clink glasses before I drill her again. "Why are you shy around food?"

"I'm not," she denies vehemently. "I ate all mine and half of your fries last night."

"Good point. But you were also going to settle for a banana."

"Nice volley, Dan." Sighing heavily, she confesses, "Gary considered me fat, and he found it unappealing to watch me eat."

"You got brass ones, my sweet lady, to tell me a truth like that. You're the bravest and most generous person I've come across in a long time. You are not fat." I speak each word like a complete sentence, ensuring she hears what I'm telling her. "I could watch you bake and eat and drink for the rest of my life. Your every move is sexy, sensual, and feminine. And that includes every square inch of your perfectly formed figure." I don't give her any space to be embarrassed or counter my declaration. "Do you have any idea what we're celebrating today?"

She shakes her head, her pale skin turning crimson and hiding her freckles. She's pleased with my honesty.

"Today is the first day of what I hope will be many dates. Weekends spent outdoors eating, drinking, and dancing— weeknights doing the same indoors. Then, traveling abroad and making love at every opportunity in all of those places. You in?" I raise my glass again, hoping she'll agree to my terms, but she's shaking her head again.

"I could never allow myself to fall in love with a smoker." Her eyes dart to my shirt pocket, where the pack shows through.

"What is it, the smell?"

"My father passed away from COPD. I can't watch someone I love die that way again."

"This feels like a test." My chest tightens from desire— not for Clara, but for a final puff of heavenly, harmful smoke. The cravings will only get worse. I might as well get used to them now. "You know what? I want the girl. I don't need the butts." Pulling the pack out, I crush the box and toss it with the lighter into the breadbasket. "Done. I quit." I tap my foot and cross my fingers, waiting to see whether I passed or not.

"There's one other problem. I can't dance, Dan." Her eyes twinkle, and I know she's smitten too.

"Me either. We'll learn together."

"Then yes, I'm in."

We seal the deal with a kiss over the water.

6

DAN

*I*t's been less than a day since quitting smoking. Still, it's frustrating to be winded after one short game of volleyball. Greg is naturally athletic like his father, making it seem like I'm playing with my brother again. He looks so much like Mason, and their laugh is indistinguishable. On some level, it's like Mason returned from the great beyond, only less aggressive and angry. A different form, no doubt, but the energy level and the competitive streak are all from my side of the family.

"Do you swim, Uncle Dan?"

"I dog paddle."

"They teach you that in veterinary school?"

"Yeah. It's a first-semester requirement."

Laughing, we make our way down to the water to join in the frolic with Clara, Kristof, and Ryder. All three are soaked and sandy with cheerful grins on their faces. Kristof swims almost perpendicular to the water, only his hips and tail submerged. Ryder, he's your gold medalist, paddles circles around Kristof and Clara, who prefers a slower-paced butterfly stroke.

Greg and I dive under immediately, cooling off after the exertion of the game. I re-create the famous *Jaws* scene on Clara, scaring her after I grab her from below and begin gnawing on her bare torso. She looks fantastic in a flouncy black bikini—the ruffles rather becoming on her curvaceous body.

"Dan! Don't do that." She smacks the water angrily between us and laughs. "I could have drowned."

"Don't splash me, woman." I rush her and pick her up before she can react and toss her bum first back into the tide. The waves are perfect for body surfing, of which Greg and the pups are already taking advantage. I take advantage of my sputtering new friend. Helping her wipe her drenched locks from her sun-kissed face, I press my mouth over her salty lips, taking our breath away.

"You can't do that," she warns in a breathy tone.

"I just did."

"I could plot revenge."

"Or I could just kiss you again." I've convinced her.

Clara rises onto her tiptoes to draw my head down to her level before wrapping one chilly calf around my leg, and I draw her closer. Too bad she has other plans. Before I can taste her again, she pulls with her leg and pushes with both hands, and I'm head underwater.

Looking as if she might run, like maybe she *should* run, I lift her body, bringing us face to face. "Wanna make up?" I nibble on the side of her neck, tasting sun and sea, and it's got me ready to feed.

"Only if you promise not to throw me in again."

I hold her higher above the water and consider doing just that, making her squeal and struggle. Instead, I place her back down to the ground. "Your wish is my command."

She quirks one eyebrow, unconvinced.

"What? I put you down, and I've quit smoking. What else does my Clara want?"

"Lunch."

"You read my mind. Let's go." We hold hands and head up to the blankets. "Greg, you hungry?" I call out, passing the splashing trio. Neither pups nor man needs convincing. They shake off the excess water simultaneously and beat us to the picnic basket and blanket.

My audience watches with concern while I rub an antibiotic cream on my burns and cover the wounds with a towel. The skin will still be sensitive for a while, and I baby my legs to allow healing with little tissue shrinkage.

"Is it painful?" Clara adjusts the cooler and my essentials, allowing me easy access to what I need.

"No." I lie and squeeze her hand. "Thanks for your concern, though. Let's eat!" I serve up plates of fried chicken, potato salad, and potato chips, doling out beer to Clara and myself and water to Greg and the thirsty mutts. Kristof and Ryder sit patiently, awaiting anything offered, like treats or fallen pieces of food. They sit side by side, rigid with attention.

"What a perfect beach day," Clara exclaims as we tuck into the simple meal.

The sun is hot and high in the sky, and the water is cool enough to bring down core body temperatures yet not so much that a person can't stay in it and play a while. The sandy beach isn't too crowded, and the seagulls are off doing something other than scouting for our meal.

"You can't beat the company, that's for sure." I tip my bottle to them both before taking a sip. "It's been great getting to know you, Greg. You're just like Mason." I rush to reassure him, knowing he's familiar with Mason's troubled side. "The good parts. The best, truly."

"What was he like? I mean, Jack tells me a lot, and I don't know…" He trails off, looking at the surf. "I guess I can never hear enough about him." He tries to hide the pain, the way a nineteen-year-old will, but we all know growing up without both parents is difficult. "It was one of my biggest dreams that someday I would get to meet him."

Clara rubs his back gently and hands him a big slice of chocolate cake she made just for the occasion. "It's terrible that you didn't get to meet your dad. Not fair." He rests his head briefly on her shoulder. She has this way about her that makes people feel comfortable and relaxed. After the year I've had, I can't believe my luck in meeting her.

"Come on, Dan, tell him your favorite Mason moment." Clara sets me up for storytime.

"Limiting me to only one is going to be tough. Are we talking G-rated, or can you handle tales of Mason's rebellious streak?"

"I think Jack sticks to the happy stuff, but he was a whole person." Greg shrugs. "I want to know it all."

I don't want to freak the kid out by describing how some of the people who picked a fight with my combative brother looked after a severe pummeling, and I choose an anecdote one could define as a middle-ground escapade for Mason. "My parents weren't prepared for Mason. Gabe and I were trouble, but in a more conventional sense, like egging a house or two on Halloween. Driving into the yards of people we felt had wronged us, leaving thick grooves of mud in their pristine lawns. Drinking and partying in the woods. Things like that."

"My mom didn't let me do any of that stuff," Greg jokes.

"I hear that. My mother tried, she did, but four boys? And the youngest twins? No, she had her hands full from the start. Plus, I bet you were more like Jack. Jack was always patient and slow to anger. He could usually hold his own in a fight, but talking things out was his preference. Schooling was his priority from the start."

"Yeah. Sometimes I pretend Jack is my dad because they're identical, and I connected with him almost instantly."

Clara is at it again, thrusting more comfort food and another water bottle into Greg's hands. He's a wall of athletic muscle and will burn off the loving calories probably in seconds.

"I bet Jack loves that, Greg," Clara tells him sweetly, and I continue on about Mason's troubling time in military school.

"My parents decided to close rank and take a firm stance on Mason's behavior. After being arrested a second time for spraying graffiti on the town water tower, they threatened Mason with military school. He told them if they forced him to go—and he would never go willingly—he'd figure out a way to escape. They could toss their tuition money down the drain for all the good it would do them.

"My parents didn't listen. Maybe they felt it was too late, the threat already made. Mason got busted for buying marijuana in an age where that sort of thing was illegal, and they made good on their warning, sending him straight to the hellish institution." I laugh when another memory pops up. "That's right. The night he smoked it, he stayed at a friend's house. Mason was stoned and couldn't sleep. He snuck quietly into the basement to listen to some music on their state-of-the-art stereo system. He plugged in the headphones, cranked them to their highest volume, and sank back into the worn leather sofa to chill.

"Almost immediately, he was pushed from the chair, the earbuds were pulled out, and his friend's mother was screaming in his face. He hadn't pushed the adapter for the headphones in tight enough. The music blared, and he woke the entire family to heavy, death metal music. Scared the bejeezus out of them."

The two of them think it's funny too. While we're distracted, Ryder jumps in and snags the last drumstick. It's a three-way tug between Ryder, Kristof, and me for the chicken bone. Thankfully I win and place them in a sit position, allowing them to share the spoils—except for the lethal bone—and wrap up the remains of anything readily accessible to an ever-attentive dog.

Returning to the main story, I wipe the dog slobber from my hands onto my swim trunks. "Us three brothers missed him terribly. Mason was a troublemaker, but he was also funny and loving, at least to us. He only came home once or twice that first semester. Anyone could tell by looking at him he was even harsher, angrier. He told my parents of the abuse the boys were suffering at the hands of the headmaster. They reframed it as the discipline Mason sorely lacked. They were way off. Eventually the school closed down due to the injustices committed by the son of a bitch. The headmaster died not long after Mason. It may not be right, but I still wish Mason had had the opportunity to pummel the freak."

Clara sees I'm getting upset and hands me cake.

Noticing the smaller slice, I can't help asking, "Hey, why is Greg's serving bigger than mine?"

Her eyes slip down to my waistline.

"I saw that! Are you judging me?"

"Well," she begins haltingly. "You've been eating an awful lot of desserts these past couple of days."

"What? I had a little cake and a few brownies. You made them for me."

"I made three dozen, and they're all gone. You can't trade

addictions, Dan. You just quit smoking, and it's okay indulging a little. But that's a lot."

Greg tries to cover his mirth behind his half-pound slice. "She's right. You look like you have the tendency to go soft." He buffers his words. "Like in the off-season."

"I guess my diet starts today." I hand Clara back the cake untouched.

"Oh, baby, don't be that way. I'll feed you cake every day —by the slice. Okay?" She breaks off a piece with her fingers and feeds me.

"Fine." Soothed, I agree to her terms, feeling the rich frosting melt in my mouth. With my sugar fix back in hand, I continue.

"Mason was newer to the school than other classmates and the lowest man in the pecking order. His job was to stand guard while the others broke into the headmaster's house to steal whatever they could get their hands on. I suspect the reason they went at night was to get caught on the first try. It assured expulsion, and it worked like a charm. Mason came home. The parents were pissed. It went down just as he predicted. They lost a good ten grand, and he lost the ability to trust them again.

"I'm not blaming anybody. People do their best, most of the time. But I don't think—" I shake my head ruefully. "No, I know military school did nothing to make Mason a better person and only added to his natural tendency towards the morose, feeding a need for revenge." I pat my pocket for a cigarette and remember I quit—and I'm not wearing a shirt.

"Bottom line, people might judge a person like Mason and label them 'bad' or 'antisocial,' but sometimes you find a person who might need a bit more understanding, be shown a little extra attention, or be given a break now and again."

Clara chimes in with her own opinion based on her experience. "And sometimes it still isn't enough. Gary will never rehabilitate." I kiss her on one cheek while Greg pecks her on the other. She's got us both eating out of the palm of her hand.

"Technically, neither did Mason."

We're in agreement over the sentiments. Three people with similar perspectives converge where the evidence speaks for itself. People make choices based on what they know, and it doesn't mean those decisions are in the best interest of themselves or others. You can't escape destiny, and none of us makes it out alive.

7

CLARA

*D*riving away from the service station was a lot harder than expected. Watching Dan wave forlornly in the rearview as I went, it took all my strength to keep going. Frankly, I left more for myself than for him. He begged me to stay last night after the beach and again this morning over my freshly made raspberry Danish.

"Clara, we don't know whether Gary will post bail or not. It could be dangerous, going home this soon," he had argued between massive bites of the pastry. I remember wondering, did he eat that way all the time, or is it from quitting smoking?

Dan's been eating whatever was in sight the last few days, mainly the stuff containing lots of sugar and butter. When I called him out about it at lunch yesterday, it had really been a joke. He's almost as lean as his nephew, and Greg is an avid cross-country runner. Greg has the body type I would sell my firstborn to have inherited. Oh, to be one of those flapper gals!

During our argument about my moving home, I tried explaining to Dan how Gary hasn't worked a real job in five years. He had countered with my earlier share that Gary had briefly sold drugs off-island. Dan's point was that Gary survived somehow and that massive cash flow is hard to give up.

"I know." I patted his hand and gave him another slice of Danish while pouring him a second cup of coffee. "I have Kristof to protect me, and my neighbor, Mrs. Ridley, is always around. You met her at the senior center."

He balked at the news. "What! Isn't she eighty?"

"Eighty-five, so clearly fit for her age and more than capable of dialing 911. She's a sweetheart who has helped me more than once." I didn't tell him then that I meant "Helped me eat the leftover baked goods." The less he knows, the better. We bickered back and forth until I threatened him with shutting off the sugary snack supply.

"Whoa," he exclaimed, pushing away from the table, taking the remaining tart with him. "That was uncalled for. I'll take you to pick up your car, but you have to promise to come back."

"With dessert?" I surmised.

He pulled me onto his lap swiftly and began licking the length of my neck. "You're my favorite treat—just you will more than suffice." Continuing to sample the product, he reconsidered, afraid I'd believe his fib. "In case I've confused the situation, I wouldn't slam the door on a hot-from-the-oven apple pie."

We both laughed, and Kristof barked to join in the fun.

Now that I've arrived home, I miss our argument. It's lonely carrying my new things into the apartment and opening all the windows without Dan hovering.

I can't help but notice how the clothes he bought me make all my other outfits look shabby and worn. I need to figure out a way to expand the business going forward.

Already I'm cooking at least eight hours a day and making deliveries after, and it hardly leaves time for doing much else. Maybe I'll make some flyers and hang them around the town square this afternoon. Businesses are open for the season, and I'm bound to get a few calls.

Dan can't bankroll my entire life after knowing each other only a few days. He wouldn't even listen to my ideas for a payment plan on my car repair. "No, Clara. It's already paid," he said after retrieving his credit card from the repair shop assistant, and that was that. He walked me to my car and waved me off.

The car will need replacing before too long, and these tattered textiles have got to go. When we head out for the date nights he described, I'd like to be wearing something without holes, tears, or fading.

Making good on his other promises, he danced me around the kitchen during my last night at his place to the slowest songs we could recall. We did a terrible job. I don't know which of us had more bruises, but, wow, did we ever laugh. I never had a moment that free and silly with Gary—not even close.

Now that I've checked in with Mrs. Ridley to let her know I've returned, I need to stop daydreaming about Dan and focus on more serious business. I sit down at the computer to create a business sign that will leave people drooling and desperate for one of my creations.

Dan

Jonesing for a smoke, I take myself out for a walk on the beach instead. I have to get those breathing exercises in one way or another. If I can't have a cigarette, and I promised to give Clara "space," then I've no choice in staying busy.

The sand has the right amount of squish to it, and I remove my sneakers to feel it between my toes, and I walk the shore's length. I often think about Mason at the beach. It was the last place we all had fun together before it all started slipping away. We came here annually for vacation until the summer of Mason's short stint in military school. The tuition put a dent in the vacation fund that year, and afterward, my parents weren't interested in entertaining us. It was probably the right call. With the six of us in a tiny cottage, things would have gotten violent fast if we had ever had a peaceful start. And we all know long car rides with kids create the most classic memories from the unpleasantness.

Before we hit puberty, we had a blast. I don't remember ever wearing more than a bathing suit and flip-flops for the entire week. Every moment was an adventure, looking for caves along the shore, catching fiddler and hermit crabs to see how many we could find before tossing them back into the surf so we could head into town, walking miles to get an ice cream sundae. That was living.

Then the teen years came, and testosterone ruled. I can't keep from laughing at the cocky group of peacocks we were, strutting around like we were the kings when we were just naive kids. Adolescents have a way of making everything about "them" and fail to enjoy the things that matter.

It took me a long time to get to that place of enjoying things again. Once we lost Mason and I left home for good, it began to make sense. With no one to distract me, I went back to school, attained my doctorate in veterinary science, and opened the practice. I often dated in pursuit of Mrs. Right, and she never came. Women like doctors, but they don't always care for the number of hours, even less so when your patients are animals.

I know it's quick, and I likewise know Clara gets it—I only want to be with her. All the hoops she's had to jump through to keep Kristof safe are admirable. I'd like to convince her to stay with me, but, understandably, she wants to slow things down. I promised to give her until Friday before I see her again, and it's likely to be the death of me. They say absence makes the heart grow fonder. My wish is that before too many date nights pass, Clara feels enamored like me.

The look in Gary's eyes was that of a dead fish. I don't like to think about it and reach for my non-existent ciga-rettes again. I need a fix and recognize I'm closer to town than to the cottage. Relying entirely on memory, the ice cream parlor should be two streets down on the right. I pick up the pace as the sandy ground turns into a cobblestone sidewalk.

Clara

I tack up my last flyer on the souvenir store and plan to treat myself to a hot fudge sundae. Kristof is panting beside me, vying for his own dish of vanilla soft serve.

The gift shop owner said he'll be ordering a cake for his daughter's pre-school graduation. She wants a mermaid design, and I consider including Dan in the process and then decide I'd prefer to get paid than be made to laugh. He's always doing that anyway. Dan is quite the clown once he's relaxed. With his easy-going nature, it's understandable why animals take to him so quickly. There must be something good in the Bryant Brother's blood. Kristof liked Greg from the start, the same way he did Dan.

No one can usually get near me with Kristof around, except for Brandon. Even Gary, more often when he drank, could barely get within three feet of the dog. I still don't understand why he was adamant about taking Kristof—they despised each other. Gary hates Kristof because Gary hates everything, and Kristof is afraid of unpredictability. Plus, Gary is a shit and dogs cue into that personality defect with ease.

Turning in the direction of the ice cream shop, I'm bumped into a streetlight post by someone quickly turning the corner. "Excuse me!" The man grabs me by the shoulders to prevent me from stumbling over the concrete base. "Hey, I know you."

"Dan, you promised," I admonish him before I allow him to brush his lips against mine. I like the tingly feeling he creates under my skin wherever he touches me.

"In my defense, you did get," he looks down at his watch, "five hours alone before running into me. That's sorta like three days in dog time."

Dan holds his hand low, and it seems Kristof gives him a high five in solidarity as he taps it with a paw.

"Liar!" I smack his arm lightly to temper the accusation. "We agreed to three human days."

"You dictated the amount of time I should spend pining. I'm just Danny-go-along. Besides, this was completely unplanned and spontaneous. I'm trying to get you off my mind by staying busy."

"Oh? What have you been thinking?"

"I could tell you, but showing you will be much more fun." He twirls me into a narrow alley between the two stores, stepping on all my toes. We're groping each other like we're the first people to discover carnal desires, and I can't remember why I wanted this much "me" time in the first place. Sooner than I'd like, Dan pulls back, panting the same as me, and adjusts the front of my rumpled blouse, buttoning it high enough to cover the lace bra he just exposed to any rats that might be hiding behind the dumpster. "This may not be the most romantic place, but you did want to know. Now, are you going to let me buy you an ice cream cone or not?"

"I was going to have a sundae." I brace myself, still prepared for a Gary comeback.

"Even better. I'll have one too." He takes me by the hand and leads me to the order window and then under a shade tree to enjoy the snack. Kristof has his bowl licked clean in no time and lies down to rest after having a drink of water. The breeze is warm and light, and life feels right. We chat and laugh, and Dan walks me to my car once we're finished, insisting he will obey the rules from now on. "Unless you follow me again, Clara. I can't factor in for your stalking ways."

If only I recognized the foreshadowing in his words. Maybe it would have changed things.

8

DAN

*H*ow can three days feel like an eternity? How many miles have I tread on the beach, and how many times have I bothered my nephew for a cup of milk or sugar, knowing he didn't have it and I didn't need it? Too many to keep track of, but better than wasting time pining over Clara. She's not gone, only cautious.

My spare time has helped me decide my future, and it's clear I can't go back to California. Healing from the ordeal has to be the priority, and recovery from the psychological wounds will take longer than the third-degree burns on my legs. The tissue no longer needs debriding, which is a bonus. Still, the pain lingers, the rawness a constant reminder of all that went horribly wrong.

A group from the county where the veterinary medical center sits recently placed a full-page letter asking me to come back in the local newspaper. They included signatures from the pet owners who lost a companion in the fire to assure me that there was nothing to forgive. It will take a long time to integrate the message as my truth, and I can't thank them enough for their support. I wish starting over there was an option, but it's not. Seeing the old site whenever I drove past would invariably keep all my internal wounds fresh.

Here, in Bristlemouth Bay, a future can be had. I'm unwilling to grow a gigantic practice like the old place. Keeping the clinic on the island will guarantee the size remains manageable. I'll get closer to my family and, as importantly, work towards making Clara a new member. She may not know it yet, but she is the "one."

Tonight, we're heading up to Boston for an off-island date. She'll find the package I left on her doorstep soon, and I hope she likes the dress as much as I do. It's her choice to wear it or not, but with her budget tight, I wanted to give her the option of wearing something brand new. She could wear a burlap bag and still look incredible, in my opinion. From what I've gleaned about women, it's not the style most are looking for, going out for dinner and dancing, which is why I played it safe and asked for professional input. We'll have our first dance lesson tonight—the cha-cha—and the black dress will flare just enough to make the moves attainable. At least that's what the boutique owner where I bought it told me.

Strolling towards her apartment, I stop into the local florist shop to pick up a box of chocolates and a bouquet of daisies. The cold smell of "funeral" accosts me, and I'm forced to mouth-breathe while exchanging pleasantries with the owner. I fight the image of Mason in the last moments of his life and those horrible days spent staring at him in the open casket during his services and launch my way back onto the sidewalk, pushing the door harder than necessary, almost taking it off the hinges.

Whew! It takes a few minutes to get my head back on straight. Leaning against the cool brick building to stop the darkness from seeping further into my psyche, I remind myself that tonight is not about the past. My attention faces forward where a bright new future awaits. Clara's smiling face comes to mind, and I'm marginally better.

Continuing on to her place, I quicken my pace. Still, my ruminations are dark. Why would a lovely woman like Clara put up with abuse from such a waste of a human? Gary is pond scum, and the faster they can get him off-island and into a prison cell, the better the world will be.

"Uncle Dan!" Greg's voice interrupts my imaginings of all the bad things Gary will face once he receives a sentence.

"Hey, Greg! Good to see you. What brings you to town?"

He's out of breath and struggles to get the words out. I've seen Greg run plenty; he doesn't get winded.

"Slow down. Take a couple of deep breaths, and then tell me what's going on."

His skin color goes from plum to red to pink, leaving him enough oxygen to talk. "I heard it on the police scanner. Gary got into another fight. He stabbed his cellmate with a plastic fork, and the cop on duty responded to the noise. Gary stabbed him in the eye, grabbed his gun, and ran out the back. They put out an all-points bulletin. You mentioned seeing Clara tonight, and I ran as fast as I could."

"When?" I grab him by the shoulders and shake him out of fear.

"Another call went out ten minutes ago. Gary took off an hour ago."

"Okay. Come with me and stay across the street. Call the police and tell the dispatcher that we're afraid Gary might come looking for Clara." I change my mind. "No, insist that she's in danger. They have enough to worry about, but it's likely the case. Can you do that?"

Greg already has his phone in hand, and he crosses the street. He can hide safely behind the mausoleum in the small graveyard by the church in case Gary comes sniffing around.

The man is armed to the teeth, and with Jack and Colleen out of town, Greg's safety is my responsibility. Trying to keep panic in check, I jog up Clara's stairs, enter the building, and tap lightly on her door.

Clara

Kristof has been panting and whining all day. He gets like this sometimes when he knows I'll be away for a short time. It must be the dress that gave it away. We both tripped over it after we returned from our afternoon walk behind St. Stephan's. Even though Gary is locked away, if I'm alone outside with Kristof, I play it safe by sticking to the one spot in Bristlemouth Bay Gary always avoided, the heathen.

Speaking of which, I can't help check myself out in the mirror again. Pride is one of the seven deadly sins, and Dan knows my taste incredibly well. Arguably, better than I do, for I'd never have believed such a design would look good on my curvy figure. Gary couldn't guess my eye color, even if they're brown like most of the world's population.

Kristof locks eyes, pleading with me in the mirror and yelps, and I question whether it was a mistake not asking Brandon to pet sit. It's too late now. Dan will be here soon, and I left my earrings in the bedroom. The bathroom is set up comfortably with water, Kristof's plush new bed, and his favorite chew toy. The dim light and small space will help him feel safer. After the extra long walk we took, he should fall asleep shortly after I leave.

"You'll be okay. Be a good boy, and remember, mommy loves you."

The door snicks closed, and a steel grip takes me by the

shoulders and throws me into the opposite wall. Bright red blood spurts from my nose, soiling the white paint before dripping down my neck towards my exposed cleavage. Before I have a chance to wipe the gore away, Gary's fist crashes into my cheek, knocking me to the ground. I reach for the doorknob to let Kristof out. He's going berserk, barking and scratching the paint. He'll kill Gary if I can just open the door.

The blood makes my hand too slippery to grasp tight enough to twist the knob. Gary kicks me in the side to stop me, and I feel a rib crack and give up the struggle. We're alone, and he told me that there were only two reasons he would ever come back when we broke up for good. One, to get Kristof, and two, to kill me. Gary never believed the evidence I tried to create by keeping his dog hidden and on the move. He laughed uproariously at that second reason because he would kill me if he found me with Kristof anyway. He called me stupid and pointed out why he found it hysterical, saying, "Either way, you'll pay with your life."

Gary kicks me again, and I'm relieved he lands on the soft tissue of my leg until the muscle spasm and the pain elevates to an excruciating level. It hurts enough to take away the horror of my broken face, if only for a moment.

It's a struggle to use my voice and buy some time. The taste of blood makes me gag, and I hock a clot from the back of my throat onto the floor to clear it. "Gary, how did you get out?"

He always bragged about how smart he was…how, if he ever got arrested, it would be easy to find a way to escape. Shame on me for not believing such a thing was possible outside of Hollywood.

Gary pulls my head back by the roots of my hair to look me in the eyes. It's on the tip of my tongue to ask him what color they are, but it's more important for the kicking to stop.

"I told you a thousand times, Clara. I'm smarter than them, and I'm smarter than you too."

"I know, Gary. But why?" My head falls heavy, dropping suddenly after he rips his fist from my hair, tearing chunks off in the process. The clumps drop feather-light into my lap.

"Why what?" He rifles through my purse, taking the scant few bills inside, along with my car keys.

"Why do you hate me this much?" I don't care, but I could swear I heard a knock at the front door. I can't scream for help until I'm sure.

"That's a stupid question. See?" He laughs at how he just validated his point. "I guess that's it, Clara; you're stupid. Not to mention fat and useless and ugly."

Someone *is* at the door! Both Gary and Kristof hear the sound, too. Kristof wildly slams himself against the wood. Gary snatches my hair in another death grip, strong enough that my bum raises off the floor for a moment like I'm being levitated by the devil. He commands, "Get them to go away. Now!" his voice low and menacing.

"Who's there?' I call out, trying to sound normal with a throat filled again with phlegm and blood from my injured nose.

"It's Dan, Clara."

"Hi, Dan. Maybe you could come back in half an hour? That would be great."

"I think we agreed to five o'clock."

Gary rolls his hand in a "Let's get this wrapped up" gesture.

"We did. But the lemon meringue pie you ordered hasn't cooled enough for boxing up yet."

I encourage Gary to keep his eyes on me by lunging for

the bathroom door. Forget my hair at this point. More bald spots are a small price to pay for freedom from this maniac. Either Kristof gets out of the bathroom or Dan has a chance to come inside the apartment, then I might be safe from further injury and danger. It all hinges on whether Dan understood my clue about the pie.

Gary finally lets go of my hair only to grab my arm and twist it behind my back, high enough that the tips of my fingers reach my neck. My wrist snaps at the old injury site, and I scream in agony.

Gary gets thrown to the floor beside me, and Dan knocks him out with one punch. Dan pulls his fist back and realizes no further blows are necessary, and the bathroom door swings wide. Kristof latches onto Gary's throat, shaking him furiously.

"Off, Kristof!" I command authoritatively, though it hurts to speak.

It's not Gary I'm worried about, but my dog. He can't kill my ex without paying with his own life, and I'm keeping Kristof, no matter what happens.

Kristof stops his attack, awaiting further direction. Kristof follows at Dan's heel after Dan sweeps me up and carries me to the sofa. Dan holds me in his lap while Kristof attempts to administer first aid by licking my face clean.

"The police are on the way. Greg's been waiting outside for them to arrive. He'll come in once things settle down and take care of Kristof, then I can take care of you." He kisses me gently on top of my head, soothing me with the sound of his voice. "Gary is never going to hurt you again, sweetheart."

"How can you know? He got out once, and he can do it again."

I can't fight the tears with a broken rib and allow them to

flow. Kristof doesn't mind the extra saline. "I've ruined everything! Just when I finally found happiness."

"Shhh. Nothing's ruined."

He and Kristof cock their heads to the side like a mirror image. "Hear that? The police will be here in no time."

The sirens cut off, and before we hear boots on the stairs, Gary begins to stir.

"Stay where you are, asshole!" Dan stands, placing me on the cushion behind him to protect me with his body. "You're too late. The cops are coming."

We can hear them running up the stairs, radios squawking, turned up high.

"You're fucking dead, you bitch!" Gary barrels down the hall with a revolver in his hand. Time slows, and all I hear is my heartbeat. He bursts into the living room, lifting the gun, centering it at Dan's chest, and a shot fires.

But it's Gary who falls to the floor. The first officer to enter the apartment holsters his discharged firearm, and the two behind him secure the area. Firefighters and paramedics fill the rest of the space in the small room. One man dressed in a white shirt and blue pants tends to me, and another checks Gary's vitals. With one hand on Gary's pulse and the other lifted to look at his watch, the paramedic announces, "Time of death 5:05 p.m."

"It's all over, Clara. You're safe."

Wrapped once again in Dan's strong embrace, I know it to be true.

9

DAN

*D*iagnosis: death, and just like that, Clara and Kristof are free. Without the right words to express my relief and gratitude, I sit silently, watching the medic readying Clara for transport, calming her fears about resetting her broken bones.

"He did a number on you, ma'am, but the doctors and nurses will know what to do. Don't worry about a thing. We're going to take good care of you until then, okay?"

Clara nods bravely and gently to avoid further pain.

"Now, we'll need you over on the stretcher." The guy stares at me.

"I have to let you go for a moment, sweetheart." With the other medic still occupied with Gary while he awaits the medical examiner, an ambulance attendant helps cover her to the chin with a blanket and straps her to the stretcher. "You can follow us, sir. Strict rule, only patients allowed inside the ambulance.

Panic darkens her face. "It's okay. They're professionals, sweetheart. I'll be right behind them. Promise." I kiss her lips gently and let them take her away.

I hold Kristof by the collar. He tries to lunge forward, both of us thinking alike. *I'm not leaving my woman.* "Sorry, buddy. They pulled rank."

My nephew stumbles into the room with eyes wide in surprise from the events.

"Ah, Greg, you got past the melee."

"It's crazy outside, Uncle Dan. Cars can't even get down the street with so many fire trucks and police cruisers."

"Dan? What are you doing here?" The medic who called the time of death stands behind me, gawking.

Simultaneous to asking, "Do I know you?" I turn to look at the man and see that I do. "Gabe?" I couldn't be more shocked if it was Mason standing in front of me. "Gabe?" It's unbelievable. Our missing brother has been right under our noses all this time. "You live here on the island too?" He looks good. Fit as ever with a healthy tan.

"No. Bristlemouth doesn't have a station. I have a place over the bridge in Antonville."

I pull him into a tight embrace, speechless. He was the closest person in the world to me for over two decades. We shared a room, clothes, book reports, and anything else imaginable. He clings just as tightly until it's clear the rest of his team is ready to go.

"Give me a couple of minutes," Gabe tells them. "I'll be right down." He points to me. "He's my brother." They seem to understand, and the space empties.

Greg interrupts the quiet. "Is this my Uncle Gabe?"

Gabe stares at Greg, mouth agog. "He looks like—" A small collection of tears pooling in his eyes has him at a loss for words.

"Mason." I complete the sentence for him, remembering my similar reaction the day I first laid eyes on our nephew. "This is Mason's son, Greg. Greg, meet your uncle Gabe.

And, to really blow your mind, Greg's mom Colleen is currently on her honeymoon—she just married Jack."

Tough as nails when it comes to fighting, our affection for one another has always had a way of bringing a Bryant man to the brink of tears. The three of us embrace, stumbling incoherently over questions we desperately want to be answered. None will be addressed at this meeting, for Gabe is off to another call.

"Here." He hands me his phone. We wipe off our faces, trying to act nonchalant. "Send yourself a message. I'll call after my shift ends tomorrow." Gabe gives it to Greg next. "Your's too. We've got a lot of catching up to do," he tells us, heading out the door.

"Life sure has a funny way of getting weirder, doesn't it?" With my arm around Greg's shoulders, he only nods. Digesting the events of today is going to take us all some time.

"I saw Clara on the way up. She's going to be okay, right?"

"Clara!" I almost forgot there was something even more pressing than finding my long-lost brother. "She will. Broken bones, mostly, nothing they can't fix. You sure you're up for taking Kristof?"

"Totally. Ryder will love it."

We make short work of grabbing his essentials.

After sending Greg and Kristof back to Jack's, I root through Clara's things and pick out the new items we bought. The rest can burn for all I care, and she can have every new product under the sun after she promises never to come back to this apartment of abhorrence.

ॐ

"Are you family?" The tired-looking receptionist gives me the once-over.

Why do they always ask that? What, like no one has ever watched a medical show? And we don't know we'll have to lie the moment we walk through the sliding glass doors? What is family anyway? Everything in some cases and nothing in others. The question should be, "Do you love them and prioritize their happiness and wellbeing?"

Where that answer is yes, so is my response to her question. "Yes. I'm her husband." She looks for a ring, but my hands have been in my pockets since I got here, jiggling change and keys because I'm nervous and I can't smoke. Nothing will settle me down until I see for myself that Clara is okay.

"Fine." She points to the left. "Those elevators, up to the second floor, take a right. Stop at the nurse's station and tell them who you are."

"Appreciate it!" I run, catching the doors before they can close. "Pardon me," I say to the startled couple seemingly here to have a baby. I'm not going to ask unless the baby's head begins to crown. You don't need to have sisters to know that much. We all stare politely at the elevator keys until I reach my floor and exit the small chamber.

The nurse at the desk looks exhausted too, but she's much more pleasant than the receptionist after giving her my wife's name. Hey, the future counts.

Clara is resting with her head on the pillow, facing towards the window. The view beyond the panes is nothing special to see, only another concrete wing of the hospital. Taking her hand gently so as not to wake her, I startle when she speaks. "I've been waiting for you." Her words slur with the medication.

"I had to take care of Kristof, my love, and pack a few things. Mind if I join you?"

Her face is black and blue and painfully swollen, and I've never witnessed a more beautiful sight. She's smiling. "Please." We adjust things until we're both happy with the arrangement, and it takes some doing with her lines and catheters.

"You saved me, Dan." Her face crumples, and she releases the floodgate. Pulling her close, I cradle her like a baby in my arms. She's strong and fragile and amazing for withstanding the blows the way she did.

"You did incredibly well, Clara. You're a brave survivor. We'll get through this." I patiently wipe her face until the powerful emotions she just released leave her lying limp against me.

"How did you know that Gary would be in my apartment?"

"Greg heard on the scanner that he'd escaped, and I hoped to beat Gary inside. Mentioning the pie was clutch, sweetheart. The second you said 'lemon meringue,' I knew he was with you. After I kicked the door in and saw you were struggling to let Kristof out of the bathroom, I saw red with all that blood pouring off you. He's lucky I knocked him out with one punch. I wouldn't have stopped otherwise."

"I can't believe he had a gun. He was going to shoot me."

"But he didn't. He's the one who died, and he can never hurt you again." My words have the proper impact. Clara slumps against me into a deep sleep, and I shuffle out from beneath her and spoon her close.

Clara

Three days after being admitted, the doctors released me from the hospital. Dan carries me over the threshold of his brother's rental cottage like a new bride, refusing to let me walk, even though the doctor insisted it was essential for the healing process.

"Set me up here, Dan." He gently places me on the sofa inside the three-season porch before reaching behind me for a royal-blue throw and laying it over my lap. "I want to watch the world go by now that it's safe." I've become so used to my life of subterfuge that I'd forgotten the simple pleasure of people watching and cloud gazing. The ocean air wafting in through the screens tickles my bruised and battered skin, bringing a unique brand of relief.

"Can I get you anything?" Dan hands me a glass of water and two pain pills, knowing the jostling from the car ride has my wounds singing out for comfort.

"I'd like to take a bath in a little bit if you could help me. Right now, sitting here and basking in my freedom is enough."

He pulls me close to his side, and I feel even more secure. He knows how to touch me in a way that causes no pain and comforts my soul.

"Do you want to see Kristof?"

Kristof can't be here. He's always the first to greet me the second I arrive anywhere with whines and kisses. "Where is he?"

"He's in the kitchen, waiting for my cue. We've been working on a little something."

My curiosity piqued; I need to know, so I nod.

"Kristof, come," Dan calls out.

Immediately, Kristof's dog tags rattle in response, and he bounds into the room.

"Sit," Dan tells him first. Then he commands, "Present."

"As in 'present arms,' not the gift," he explains to me with a wink.

Kristof snuffles under the couch before plopping a small box in my lap.

"So it is a present," I chide.

I tear open the ivory-colored wrapping paper and find a black velvet box. "Dan? What have you done?" My breath catches, and it isn't from my injuries.

"Open it, Clara."

I do, and he continues, "Marry me, sweetheart. Let me take care of you forever."

Stunned at the sparkle and size of the brilliant gem, I whisper, "This wasn't supposed to happen to me."

"Why not?" He strokes my hair back, playing with my sparser but still springy curls.

"I'm damaged goods."

"Nope. Those days are over. I'm never letting anyone hurt you ever again, Clara. Say yes."

Kristof places one hand on my leg, imploring me with his eyes.

"Did you teach him that too?"

Dan shrugs. "No, the smart dog figured it out himself. Please say yes," he repeats in a tone indicating he won't quit until I do.

But that's not why I say yes. "I'll marry you, Dan, because I love you."

"I love you, too, Clara." He slips the ring on my finger, kissing the area sweetly. "Oh, I almost forgot." Dan tosses a liver treat high in the air, and Kristof gets his reward.

EPILOGUE

DAN

*C*lara and I cut the ceremonial ribbon while our closest friends and relatives whoop and cheer around us, officially declaring our new veterinary clinic open for business. Kristof and Ryder lead the way through the front doors, giving the facility their official seal of approval. After jumping up to sit on the built-in waiting room seat, Clara tosses each dog a homemade peanut butter dog cookie. Our first clients munch away, pleased with the service provided.

"Congratulations, you two!" Colleen says as she and Jack rush through the door to hug and kiss us. Jack slips an envelope into my hand. "Open it later with Clara," he tells me before allowing our other guests access.

Brandon is next, shaking my hand, kissing Clara on the cheek. "Is he still being good to you?" he asks Clara before warning me, using the same threat from the day we all met, "I can still kick your ass back to California."

Clara defends my honor. "He's been wonderful, and I promise you'll be the first person I call if anything changes."

"Never," I promise them both, crossing my heart. Clara's happiness is my reason for living, and we all know it.

"I didn't think so." He postures like he won this round, laughing and making his way to the refreshment table.

"Scared?" Clara grins up at me. She loves how I let Brandon keep me in line, insisting it's good for his self-esteem.

"Only of you growing tired of me, sweetheart."

"Never, Dan."

Kissing her is my favorite pastime, and we indulge for a moment while our guests grab something to eat and drink. The night is a success, with people booking appointments beginning early Monday morning.

We still tire easily, both from the healing and our new adventure. And as the evening wanes, I sling my arm over Clara's shoulders and let her do most of the talking while my mind wanders through all the moments that brought us here. Though it took months, it's been well worth the struggle. We holed up for a time after Clara returned home from the hospital, only venturing out to pick up food or walk on the beach to aid in our recovery. Twice daily, Clara rubbed healing ointment on my burns, while as many times as I could get my hands on her (admittedly a lot—she sure is purty!) I massaged arnica cream into her bruised flesh.

While our wounds healed, our love grew, and being apart from one another became unbearable for us both. Clara is now my assistant, and I am hers. By keeping the clinic small, I can help her bake for a select clientele. I'm even allowed to help decorate, with strict rules mandating it can only be done privately once we're alone. I draw all sorts of impressionist art on her face, belly, and unmentionable bits. Last night it was a rendition of the first time we took a dance lesson. Technically, it was two stick figures holding stick fingers, smiling broadly, drawn down the length of her back, but she got the gist.

I'm in the middle of planning out tonight's masterpiece, and Clara interrupts. "More champagne, Dan?" She hands me a glass, her eyes twinkling brightly over her own flute. "Where did you go? You looked far away and happy."

"I'd call it paradise." I lean in close to whisper the rest in her ear. "I'm going to paint this magical moment on your entire body with my fingers and that buttercream frosting you made the second we get home." Her giggle is more bubbly than the champagne, making me want to blink the lights and head out immediately. Tough luck, my other brother and nephew just arrived.

Greg greets his mother and predestined stepfather first. They head our way with joyful wonder on their expressions, mimicking mine and Clara's. What are the odds that over twenty years after my brother Mason's murder, we would be standing together once again complete?

"I can't—" I begin and stop.

"I know." Jack grips my shoulder, tears misting his eyes, the same as mine and Gabe's.

"It's like having him back," Gabe speaks for us all. "As though the past doesn't matter anymore because we Bryant boys can't ever be separated by time or death. Life has a way of continuing."

Greg shakes his head, responding to our stares concentrated in his direction. "I'm not Mason, but I'm glad I'm his son. Having all my uncles around to fill in the blanks is a wish I never knew I had come true."

And that does it. The four of us hug each other tight, pulling Clara and Colleen into the fold. Not to be left out, Kristof and Ryder squirm between our legs and sit in the center of our tight-knit family circle.

§♣

Once we're finally home, I help Clara remove her high heel shoes and run my hand up the length of her shapely calf and under her dress, only stopping when she makes me.

"I've got to get out of this dress." Her hands reach in vain for the zipper. "I'm so used to my comfy clothes."

I'm way ahead of her in tugging the zipper down and pushing the gown's thin straps off her shoulders. "Pretty," I compliment her skin glowing in the moonlight as her head falls back onto my chest, allowing me a birds-eye view of her lovely torso. Her arms lift, encircling my neck, bringing my lips to hers while I continue to trace her form with my fingertips.

"I want you so much, Dan." She turns, and her delicate fingers begin working on the buttons of my shirt; the crinkling sound of paper stops her. "What's this?" She pulls the thick envelope from my pocket.

I flip it one way then the other, finding no clues. "I don't know. Jack gave it to me and said we should open it together." Watching her semi-nude body saunter towards our bedroom, I couldn't care less what's inside, but curiosity has the better of Clara—or she's trying to tease me. She likes playing games, drawing it out once I'm excited. I recognize it's also a test to dispel all the negativity Gary wanted to make her believe. It's fun convincing her of the truth; Clara is my brand of perfect.

She pulls out the first piece of paper, a one-dollar bill. Next, she removes and looks at another paper then hands it to me; it's the deed to the cottage, followed by a contract tagged to receive our signatures.

"The final is a handwritten note," she informs me.

"Really? What does it say?"

"Colleen is gifting the payment for the cottage. Please sign

the sales agreement and return it to the attorney on the enve-
lope. Be happy and well in your new home. We love you both!
Jack, Colleen, Greg, and Ryder
"P.S. Please bring the aforementioned one-dollar bill
payment to us A.S.A.P.
"P.P.S. Ignore Jack. He's trying to be funny. Put the dollar in
a scrapbook or hang it on the wall.
"P.P.P.S. Colleen is wrong. Bring the dollar."

"My goodness, that's so generous," Clara exclaims.

"Why, thank you," I tease, now fully undressed and striking a pose.

She laughs. "Yes, that too."

"Care to join me under the sheets?"

She nods and I pull her close to kiss her waiting lips. After satisfying each other, she rests her head on my chest. "You have the best family. I can't believe Jack and Colleen would give us this cottage."

"I agree, but wouldn't you like something bigger?"

"What could be bigger than having the man that I love and the dog of my heart?"

We both look over and laugh as Kristof snores away in his dog bed.

"Let's stay here forever, Dan."

I kiss her with the depth of my love and vow to stay forever with Clara, the cake maker, and her dog.

The End

THANK YOU READERS

Thank you for reading "The Cake Maker's Dog," Book 2 Bryant Brothers Novella Series. It would mean the world if you took a moment to post a review wherever you purchased the book and let others know what you think. Please visit kathleenpendoley.com, Instagram, Facebook, or Pinterest for information on new releases, blog posts, and more.

Keep reading for an excerpt of "Glitter and Grief," Book 3.

ACKNOWLEDGMENTS

After publishing *Trail of the Heart,* a new inner critic voice arose. It told me how the people in my life were humoring me and being kind, for clearly, "You can't write or tell a story."

Instead of hesitating, I allowed the detractor her opinion and continued to forge ahead. You can imagine how good it felt having beta readers who gave an emphatic "Yes!" to helping with a second and even third book.

Thank you, Mike Sicilia and Elaine Bradley. You keep coming back for more. Your input, opinion, and friendship mean a ton. I couldn't do it without you.

My sister and brother-in-law, Mary and John Kendzierski, gave me the kindest gift, selling my books in their gift shop at The Inn at Ellis River, their B&B nestled in the mountains of NH—thank you!

My heartfelt thanks to Jamie Ross for sticking with me, creating the prettiest book covers on earth, and teaching me techie things.

Stephanie Blackman from Riverhaven Books, your editing prowess is exemplary, and I know how lucky I am to have your expert eye perusing my manuscripts.

Finally, to my husband, Paul, and pups, Margaret and Townsend, thanks for making sure I get off the couch and out of my imaginary worlds, for reality is the place I grow.

ALSO BY KATHLEEN PENDOLEY

Bryant Brothers Novella Series

Beachy Keen Book 1

Glitter and Grief Book 3

A Nautical Twist. Book 4

Novels

Trail of the Heart

New in 2023

Confidence Quest - Pick up where you left off in *Trail of the Heart* with another adventure story, including characters known and new.

Updates at www.kathleenpendoley.com

"GLITTER AND GRIEF" EXCERPT

Chapter 1
Alicia

Little on earth holds the same gratification as that moment the most daunting item on your to-do list gets checked off so you can sit and relish in a hot mug of fresh coffee. My fingertips may burn from the many skin cells lost using the hot glue gun and the packing tape, but the autumn wreath orders are ready to be shipped on my way to meet Flora for lunch today. I should send her a text before I leave. She may forget our plans even if much of her day consists of sitting on the couch, watching her shows.

An incoming text tone alerts me. Perhaps the phone read my mind.

Can't meet today. Francine's stopping by.

Flora signs off with a heart emoji, and history indicates she won't respond to anything texted in response. It's always the same with my friend and neighbor. Any time her estranged daughter arrives out of the blue, everyone and everything else ceases to exist. It doesn't matter that Francine only has one objective—to hit Flora up for money, Flora will never stop wishing it was for more.

I return the text anyway. My mother raised me to respect others, and regardless of the painful rejection, I stopped fighting my nature long ago.

Enjoy! We'll make a date for another day soon.

My coffee tastes bitter and cold in the expected silence. I push my chair back from the kitchen island and reheat the brew in the microwave before grabbing the box of Danish pastries left over from Brandon's weekend visit home. If my son didn't love cooking so much, I wouldn't eat to the degree I've grown accustomed to. Oh, well. Diets are for tomorrow, and I need the comfort only fresh-baked love can bring today.

The first semester my son went off to college, I was sad for a short period, adjusting. Now that he's in his second year, I'm comfortable with the extra time being on my own allows. His once-a-month visits are exciting and too swift for me to get anything done, especially when he spends his time preparing my favorite foods.

The raspberry-filled Danish pairs perfectly with the caramel-vanilla-laced coffee. The jelly-like substance squirts onto my tongue, melting on contact, in perfect contrast with the crunchy, flaky crust sprinkled with sugar. It's a treat for my senses, and paired with a soft ocean breeze streaming in through the open window over the sink, I'm in my glory.

What will I do with all this unscheduled time? Without any point in stopping for lunch now that I've finished the remaining pastry, I'm left choosing between window shopping or a stroll on the beach. Or maybe I'll head off-island and take in a movie, which I haven't done since Brandon was a pre-teen. As I scroll through the phone to find out what's playing, a strange bird call breaks the solitude. Tilting my ear, I listen closer. It's a strangled sound, somehow deep and almost human. It sings in rapid succession three times as if it's calling "fire" in a rich baritone.

I shoot over to the window and throw open the sash. Things make sense now that it's obvious: it *is* a human yelling the word—a man from the sound of it.

I sniff the fresh air, and I can't see any flames or smoke shooting up from my neighbor's tiny cottage. The call continues from a nearby back yard.

It's an odd situation. My neighbor Clara told Brandon that she and Dan would still be in the Galápagos Islands for their honeymoon until later this week. Still, the yelling continues, and it seems no one else is interested in rushing to the man's aid. With my phone in hand, I head out the door to play the hero. Such a shame that I buried the cape with my husband so many years ago.

Buy "Glitter and Grief" from your favorite retailer.

Made in the USA
Middletown, DE
26 November 2022

15655491R00050